Klassic Koalas

Ancient Aboriginal Tales in New Retellings

by Lee Barwood

San Mateo, California

Other books by Koala Jo Publishing:

Klassic Koalas: Mr. Douglas' Koalas and the Stars of Qantas
Klassic Koalas: Vintage Postcards and Timeless Quotes of Wisdom
Klassic Koalas: Vegetarian Delights Too Cute to Eat
Koalas: Moving Portraits of Serenity
Koalas: Zen in Fur

A portion of the proceeds from the sales of this book will be allocated to the Australian Wildlife Hospital, a major project of Australia Zoo Wildlife Warriors Ltd. To find out how you can make a difference and support Wildlife Warriors, the wildlife conservation charity established by Steve and Terri Irwin, please visit **www.wildlifewarriors.org.**

Acknowledgments: The publisher wishes to thank Michael Hornby and Gail Gipp from Wildlife Warriors, Nick Bell from Australia Zoo, and the staff of the Australian Wildlife Hospital for carrying on Steve Irwin's legacy. Special thanks go to Lee Barwood, Donna Boiman, and the kids of the Central Ohio Art Academy for helping make this book possible.

Table of Contents

Preface

When one contemplates retelling of stories that belong to an ancient people, there are many things to be considered. How much of the original structure does a writer keep? How does that writer find the voice to tell new versions of something far, far older than herself?

And above all, why does a writer tell a story not her own?

The books and websites cited in the bibliography have all helped me to find the structure of these tales ancient before the sailing of Cook or even of Columbus or Leif Ericsson. Some of these sources contain retellings, too, that brought the voices (and in some cases, prejudices) of their authors, along with some non-Australian elements, to stories that guided original Australians in their quest for wisdom and their desire to explain the wonders of the world around them. I chose to keep the bones of the stories, in some cases paring them of elements that did not seem to belong, and in others adding elements that would make the tales my own interpretation—as has been the tradition in oral storytelling since there have been stories and tellers to tell them.

The voice is my own, developed through years of telling other stories—many based on folklore and traditions of various nations, but all made of the whole cloth of imagination.

And the desire to tell these stories comes from one thing: A love affair with the koala.

When I was perhaps a year old, I was given a stuffed koala sent from Australia during World War II by my father for one of my sisters. While stationed there, he had met the gentle koala; he brought back photographs of himself, in his Navy uniform, holding these living treasures. And he'd bought two of the toys to send to his young daughters in America, along with copies of a book telling of the adventures of Aborigine children.

Both my sisters' koalas eventually became mine, and in time my father bought me my own, also sent all the way from Australia—as well as my own copy of *The Way of the Whirlwind*, the story of Nungaree and Jungaree and their quest to rescue their baby brother from the great wind that had carried him off. Although at this writing I have not been to Australia, my earliest understanding of the magic of storytelling is colored by Australian stories; my earliest memories of the animal there to comfort me on the darkest of nights are all of the koala.

Now, however, the koala and many other wonderful Australian animals are in trouble from global warming, habitat destruction, and the incursions of predators not native to Australia. Their time may be coming to an end, as drought and fire and deforestation take their toll. So I offer these tales to try to remind us all that animals and birds have as much of a right to a safe and continued existence as we ourselves do—and in an attempt to preserve the wonder that I knew as a child when I first met that most magical of Australian animals, the koala. Each purchase of this book will make a contribution to the welfare of the animals in Australia—so this is my chance to give back in gratitude, in however small a way, for the joy, comfort, and magic that Australian animals, most particularly the koala, have given me since my earliest memories.

Thank you for giving me the opportunity to do this, and please be mindful of the needs of all the creatures of this earth. In 1854, in another wisdom tradition, Chief Seattle spoke from his heart when he reminded us that we are all part of the web of life, and we are all connected. Whatever we do to the web, we do to ourselves.

Lee Barwood
New Jersey
Christmas Eve, 2006

How the Waters Flooded the Earth

Long, long ago, in the Dreamtime, when neither men nor animals had taken their final forms, many, many creatures lived in Australia, wandering the Outback and clinging to the coasts, populating the lush valleys and sunning themselves in the hot deserts, soaring through the skies and swimming in the cool waters.

From the gentle koala to the laughing kookaburra, the hopping kangaroo and the shy wallaby, to the dingo and the crocodile and the butcherbirds and the rainbow bee-eaters, all lived in the bounty that was Australia, and they all got along tolerably well—even the Tasmanian devil, who looked and sounded far more fierce than he truly was.

But then there came a time when the soft rains failed, and the ground dried up. The blooming flowers turned brown at the edges and withered away, and the trees grew brittle from root to leaf. The sky burned down upon the flowing and still waters, drying them in a shimmer of heat, and the rocks cracked as the sun beat down. The gentle breezes changed to swift, hot winds, and scooped up the dust from the earth to carry along on their way. Those dust devils danced across the hot, dry ground and swirled high into the air, imitating their large cousins the whirlwinds as they lifted hundreds of fragile dried leaves from their resting places and tossed them skyward in a flurry of motion.

And the animals thirsted. And then they began to die.

From the creatures who lived on the land, to those who lived below it and in the deep and shallow waters, to those who dwelt in the treetops and roamed the skies, all kinds of animals and birds and fishes succumbed to the terrible drought. The Great Thirst was a massive catastrophe, and those who lived knew they had to do something even as they mourned the dead, or they would swiftly

join them. So they called a Great Corroboree in the center of the continent, and all the animals and birds left their homes and journeyed across the hot dry land to the meeting place, crawling and hopping, running and flying, walking and slithering as best they could.

When they were all assembled, they found to their astonishment a huge frog sitting in the very middle of the country. He had drunk and drunk and drunk until he swallowed up all the water in the whole continent, and he sat there fat and full of all the waters deep and shallow in the whole land of Australia. Oblivious to the other animals, he blinked in the sun, sated and glistening with moisture. Silently they sat and watched him, but he didn't move from where he sat. As thirsty as they were, the animals and birds felt hopeless to see that one creature had been so selfish as to drink up every drop.

"What can we do?" asked the duck-billed platypus, whose fur was dry. He had come a long, long way, on feet that were meant to paddle in the water, not crawl along the ground. He missed the sweet clear pool that he used to call home, with the rocks that sheltered him from the sun and the lush green vegetation that had kept him cool in its greeny-gold shadows. His leathery bill was dry and cracking. "How can we get the water back?"

The bandicoot shook his head. "I don't know. We have to ask the others. Maybe they will know." He turned to the mulgara. "Do you know?"

The little rodent shook his head and crept away to ask some of the larger animals. But the dingo didn't know either, nor did the brolga, who asked the emu, who asked the wallaroo and the possum. The Tasmanian devil snarled with thirst, but admitted that he didn't know either. He began to ask his other companions as they all searched for a solution. But neither the bilby nor the skink, who constantly flicked his blue tongue, had any idea. Neither did the bat, who spread his leathery wings and flew off to ask some of the other creatures.

The animals talked among themselves for a long time, and then they came up with an idea. The frog must be made to disgorge all the water he had drunk, so that the other creatures could survive.

And the only way to do that was to make the frog laugh. That settled, they then began to squabble amongst themselves about which animal should be the one to accomplish this.

After much heated argument, it was decided that the kookaburra, who had his own merry laugh, would try first, since laughter is infectious. So the kookaburra flew up to a branch nearby, where he could look straight at the massive frog, and where the frog could see him. He shook himself all over and fluffed his wings, then began to laugh. The other animals watched and listened, spellbound, as his voice rose from a deep chuckle to a louder and louder laugh, till the wilderness echoed and the very rocks reverberated.

But the frog simply looked at him, as if wondering what he was doing there.

The kookaburra was not used to being ignored; his laughter was contagious. The very absurdity of the idea made him laugh all the more. He laughed and laughed till he ran out of breath. Still the frog did nothing, and at last the kookaburra fell silent out of exhaustion.

The next animal to try was the frilled neck lizard. He ran up to the frog on two legs as quickly as he could, thinking that he could startle the frog into laughing. But zoom as he might, his two-legged antics did nothing to change the frog's manner. Instead the frog merely blinked. The lizard, knowing how thirsty his friends were, grew frightened; he opened his mouth to plead with the frog, and his frill unfolded and spread wide. He danced back and forth on his hind legs and waggled his frill in the air, but the frog was impassive. Dejected and despairing, at last the lizard gave up and retreated to the safety of the crowd.

The human animal came forward. She thought that perhaps if she danced gracefully enough for the frog, he might at least smile. From there she was sure she could make him laugh. She began to weave delicately back and forth, her arms and fingers tracing figures in the air, her feet tracing figures in the dusty earth. But the frog paid no attention, and she began to move ever faster and faster, at last gyrating madly and stomping her feet, raising clouds of dust that she waved away with her hands, coughing as she did so.

But even this sight was not enough to induce the frog to laugh, and at last she sank to the earth in exhaustion and despair.

When they saw this, the other animals all began to talk at once, shouting suggestions andsquabbling with each other once again. Then, driven by hunger—they had all been there quite a long time, and there had been little food to eat along their journeys—a carpet snake attempted to eat an echidna. But he forgot about the quills that made up the echidna's coat, and in horror realized that the echidna would not go down—the quills pricked him in the throat and he gagged. Suddenly he found himself being lifted high into the air—the kookaburra had seized him and was trying to fly off.

On the other side of the ring of animals, two bandicoots were squaring off over a single sweet root. As they circled each other warily, each keeping an eye on the root as well as on each other, a possum waddled up to watch. As the bandicoots flew at one another, the possum noticed the root and sidled up to it. He seized it and headed off with it while the bandicoots were fighting. Once they realized it was gone, they stopped fighting immediately and began to chase the possum, but it was too late; he had clambered up a tree, where he grasped a branch firmly with his tail and let himself down off the branch to hang upside down. Safe from the bandicoots in his airy retreat, the possum began to chew on the root, swinging gently in the breeze.

After these and a few more incidents, the animals finally stopped their arguing, and an eel surfaced from the very bottom of the river, where he lived in a deep tunnel. He swam to the edge of the water and suggested that perhaps he could make the frog laugh. The other animals, who were by now at their wits' end, agreed that he should try, so he wriggled out of the water and made his way to the frog. There he wriggled and wriggled, whipping himself back and forth with such speed that his tail hit his head again and again. When he grew tired, his wriggling slowed till it was more of a quiver that started at his head and rippled clear back to the tip of his tail, and then he jerked himself back and forth as if he were being stung by fire ants.

This got the attention of the frog, who found the sight of the wriggling eel more than he could resist. He began to tremble with contained laughter; the laughter rippled his skin from head to toe, and the ticklish sensation that resulted made him laugh aloud. He roared with laughter and the sound reverberated from mountain to mountain, along with the cheering of the animals, as the waters he had swallowed began to flow from his mouth. Out and out they poured, a trickle at first, and then swelling to a flood, swirling over the dry ground and rising, rising, everywhere pooling and flowing, until the rivers swelled over their banks and covered the land as far as the eye could see.

As the waters advanced on them, the animals quickly stopped cheering and began to cry out in fear, running and flying and swimming for their very lives. The waters rose and rose, churning and roaring, thundering down valleys and along dry riverbeds. They came more and more quickly, their turbulence crowned with a froth of white bubbles, drowning many of the animals who could not escape quickly enough, and did not stop rising until only the very tops of the mountains were visible. At last they stopped; the frog had disgorged all the excess waters he had swallowed, and swum away to his old home. And a great stillness came over the lands, broken only by the lapping of waves against the mountainsides and the occasional splash of a swimming animal.

The pelican, who at this time in the Dreamtime was not yet a pelican but a man, sailed from mountaintop to mountaintop to rescue whomever he could. On one mountaintop he found many people, and there was a woman there whose beauty captivated him. He found her irresistible, and so he began to rescue the men, several at once, each time leaving her behind. Each time she asked him why he left her, but he told her, "There is not enough room in the canoe. There are so many people to rescue, but I will come back for you." She realized quickly that what he meant to do was take her away to his own camp, and she did not want to go with him. So she found a log and wrapped it in her rug, made from the skins of possums, and then she took it to the gunyah, where he would expect her to be when he returned from his latest trip. She watched the waters recede, little by little, and as they did she followed them down from the mountaintop, finding her way to the bush.

At last the pelican-man came back and went looking for her. He called and called, but she did not answer him. Then he noticed the log wrapped in possum fur. Thinking it might be her sleeping, he touched it, then prodded it with his foot. Feeling how hard it was beneath the soft fur, he reached down and pulled the possum rug away to reveal the log. He was furious to find that she had escaped him, and resolved to find her wherever she had gone.

He bent down to a smear of white clay that the flood waters had left behind, and gathered some into his fingers; then he painted his face with it until he looked quite fearsome. Blaming the other pelican-men for the disappearance of the beautiful woman he had already thought of as his, he decided that he would avenge himself upon them. But he looked so fearsome and so strange with his white-clay-painted face that the first pelican-man he saw was terrified and struck him down with a nullah. Ever since then, pelicans have been black and white.

Gradually the waters returned to their old homes, the lakes and rivers, ponds, streams, and billabongs. Small shoots of green showed their heads above the earth, once more moist and fertile, and grew into wondrous trees and flowers. The koala was once again able to climb the gum trees, the cassowary was able to return to his beloved rainforest, and the platypus dove again into the sheltered pool. There was covering underbrush once more for the small wild things, and the breeze sang once again of tranquility and peace.

And the birds greeted the dawning sun with songs of joy and cheer.

The Koala Has Strong Arms

When the Earth was young, all things were not as they are now. In fact, Australian animals weren't yet animals at all, but men—and they didn't even live in Australia, but instead dwelt far, far across the sea, on an island where they used canoes to fish for some of their food. Yet even there they had heard of the land of Australia, rich and plump and bathed in the rays of the sun, with plenty of food for all.

There came a day when food became scarce in their island home across the sea. The animal-men all wondered what to do. They had to range farther and farther on their island to find enough food to eat, sometimes foraging late into the night by the light of the moon. And the schools of fish that had swum in the shoals just off their island swam there no longer; they had left for warmer, richer waters.

So the animal-men had to row farther and farther in their canoes to find enough fish to keep themselves fed. They were worried about what might happen if they ran out of food altogether—they had to eat, or they would all die.

And they remembered the stories they had heard of Australia, with its lush vegetation and abundant hunting under warm and clear skies. They thought longingly of this land of plenty, where food would be abundant and easy to find. Yet to get there, they would have to risk everything—they would have to journey all the way across the ocean, a vast distance much too far to swim. They would have to paddle a canoe.

Certainly they all had canoes. But most of them were normal-sized, like those belonging to Man or Crocodile, or even relatively small—like the ones owned by Starfish and Koala—and their canoes

would only hold one. But this trip would be very far, and very dangerous; many of the animal-men could not paddle as far as they would need to go, especially smaller ones like Numbat, and they would all need to depend on each other if storms blew up.

But the storms out at sea were truly fearsome. The winds would dance in the skies, growing ever faster and wilder, and then, howling in rage, they would whip the waves into a furious white froth that rose to amazing heights and came crashing down like boulders upon everything on the surface of the sea. Such storms would surely swamp the smaller canoes, or make it impossible for them to paddle in the direction of Australia; they could not risk traveling in such unseaworthy craft.

So the smaller men among them decided that what they needed was their friend Whale's canoe, because it was so large and sturdily built. Then they could all take turns paddling, and they could help each other if the seas became stormy.

There was one big problem with this plan. Whale wouldn't let anyone near his canoe, which was large and magnificent. Whale was rather selfish, and while the others would often lend or borrow things, he would not. The other animal-men talked and talked with him, first offering to bring food back to him and then trying to convince him that they would all fit in his canoe, but he wouldn't have it—first he just didn't want to share, and then he became convinced that they were just out to steal his canoe and leave him there to starve.

As they grew hungrier and hungrier, the other animal-men drew together to talk about their situation and decide what was to be done. And at last Starfish, who was a good friend of Whale, came up with a plan.

"Whale has lice in his hair," he told the others. "I look for them and take them out. But it's been a little while since I've visited him to do that. So here's what we'll do." And Starfish revealed his plan, which was to soothe Whale by looking for lice in his hair till Whale fell asleep. "While he's sleeping," Starfish said, "you get his canoe into the water, and start paddling away. I'll slip away as soon as I can and join you, and then we'll go to Australia to look for food. I know we don't want to leave him

here, but he's not changing his mind and we have to get something to eat or we'll be too weak to go at all." The others agreed.

Starfish went off to find Whale. "My friend," he said, "it's been a while since I've combed your hair for lice. How about we go to that nice quiet beach over there and I'll spend some time clearing them away for you?"

Whale agreed enthusiastically; his head was itching and he was scratching all the time. "But we have to stay by my canoe," he added. "The others have been asking about it too much, and I'm afraid that if I leave it alone they'll sneak up and take it from me."

Starfish was prepared for this. He had scouted out a place near a big hollow log close to where Whale kept his canoe. "What about this spot?" he asked, showing Whale the place he'd picked. Whale's big canoe was only a few feet away in the sand, and Whale smiled.

Whale stretched out and Starfish began picking through Whale's hair and stroking his head. As he did so, the other animal-men and Man crept up to Whale's canoe and very quietly, very slowly, began to drag it toward the water. Whale stretched and yawned, and Starfish kept working away at the lice. Every few minutes Whale would say, "Where's my canoe? Is my canoe safe?"

Starfish would pick up a stick that he had placed nearby, and he would thump with it on the log. "Your canoe is right here," he would say. "Hear this? I'm thumping on it." And satisfied, Whale would close his eyes again. Eventually Whale fell asleep and started to snore; the other animal-men moved more quickly, and got the canoe into the water and began to paddle out to sea as they'd agreed.

When Starfish saw that Whale was deeply asleep, he slipped away and ran down the beach to swim out to his friends in the canoe. But just as he'd reached the water's edge, Whale woke up and looked around for his canoe. He saw the others paddling away, with Starfish at the edge of the beach, and he let out a roar and began to run toward the water.

Desperately Starfish tried to swim out to his friends, but Whale was bigger and faster, and he caught up to Starfish in the shallows. As the others watched in horror from the canoe, Whale dragged Starfish back onto the beach and began to beat him and pummel him. "You said you were thumping on my canoe," Whale grunted. "I'll thump you!" And he did, until Starfish was very sore, and stretched every which way and very ragged and torn in appearance.

Finally Starfish cried out, "While you're beating me, they're getting away!" Whale paused for a moment, and Starfish crawled off to the shallows and hid among the rocks. Whale was furious, but realized that Starfish was right; the others were paddling madly and the canoe was getting farther and farther away. So he ran for the water and began to swim after them. Starfish, unseen, left his hiding place in the rocks and swam too. With luck, he thought, maybe he could catch up with the others and get away from the island after all.

The others paddled like mad, and Whale swam and swam. Starfish floated to the top of a large wave and was swept out to the canoe, where the others pulled him in. And Whale kept swimming.

The animal-men and Man paddled and paddled, on into the night, when they were guided by the stars high above, and all the way through till morning. Koala encouraged them when they grew tired, and his strength was an inspiration to the rest of them. They paddled all day in the hot sun and on into the next night, when the winds began to rise and howl, and the air grew chill, and the waves began to dance ominously around the canoe. But Koala cheered them and said, "I feel sure we are getting closer. Besides, we can't stop now; there is more food ahead of us than lies behind us." The others agreed, and weary as they were, they kept going even though there were no stars to guide them through this very long night. Still Whale swam, so still they paddled. They paddled through the next morning's dawn, when rains broke over the canoe and soaked everyone who wasn't already wet from the surging waves. And Whale kept swimming.

When sunset came they barely knew it; they kept paddling and paddling, because they could see Whale closing on them despite the dreadful storm. On into the night they paddled, and well into the next day, and then into the next night. One by one they began to drop of exhaustion. Finally Starfish cried, cold and miserable, "Whale will catch us, and then we'll all drown!"

But Koala, who had paddled from the beginning, reassured them. "Don't worry," he said, "I have strong arms. I will keep us ahead of Whale." And he did. His arms stroked boldly with the paddle as the storm finally lessened in intensity, and when the dawn came they saw land ahead. Koala stroked and stroked, paddled and paddled, and at last the splendid canoe bumped up against the sandy beach of that wonderful land of Australia. As the others jumped out of the canoe and ran for hiding places, Whale came up alongside the canoe and caught Koala as he tried to pull the canoe onto the shore. There he beat and hit Koala, pulling on his ears and stretching them out, and flattening his face with a direct hit to the nose.

Desperate to get away from the beating, Koala grabbed a sharp stick that was lying on the beach, and he stabbed at the back of Whale's neck, making a large hole. Whale was startled and dropped Koala, who ran for the nearest gum tree; his strong arms pulled him up and he sat there trembling in the crook of the limbs, taking the shape the koala has today. His ears stayed large, and his nose stayed flat, and his strong arms clung to the highest branch of the tree where Whale could not reach him. The still-furious Whale pulled the stick from his neck and glared up at Koala where he sat high in the tree. Whale knew he couldn't possibly get hold of Koala again, so instead he began to look around for the others; he decided once again to go after Starfish, so he jumped back into the water and breathed through the hole in his neck, which today is the whale's blowhole.

But Starfish was hiding among the rocks in the shallows, half-buried in the sand, still tattered and torn, and Whale never saw him as he swam back out into the deeper water and began to roam up and down the coast to look for him. Starfish stayed very still, so as not to attract his attention, and to this day it is easy to miss Starfish in the rock pools because he doesn't move very much.

Man, taking advantage of Whale's absence, ran back to the beach from his own hiding place and began to dance and jump on the canoe. He danced and jumped and hopped up and down with all his might and strength, breaking a big hole in its bottom. Otherwise, he feared, they would never be safe from Whale's rage; he could come ashore at any time from his canoe and beat them all up. But if the canoe were gone, and Whale stayed in the form of a whale, he would have to remain in the waters and swim for the rest of his life. When Man was satisfied that the hole was large enough, he pushed the canoe out into the water again, where it settled on the bottom; its wreckage turned into a small island at the mouth of Lake Ilawarra, where it remains to this day.

Whale had never stopped to consider that his friends wanted all along for him to leave the island with them and come to Australia. It was only his own selfishness that had kept him from joining them; they could all have traveled in safety and friendship, helping one another, on a much easier trip. But instead they all suffered through a desperate days-long chase across the stormy waters. Even now he doesn't think about the fact that, although he must stay in the water, there is plenty of food for him in his new home, and sunlight to bask in, and many new friends in the waters around the coral reefs for him to talk with.

So Whale still swims up and down the coastline, looking for the animals who were his friends on that long-distant island. The vapor still spouts from his blowhole as he swims. Koala still clings to the limbs of the gum tree with his strong, strong arms, and Starfish still hides in the sandy rock pools.

Didane and the Trees

In the Dreamtime, the Carnarvon Gorge area in Queensland was hot, and dry, and barren. The cliffs were beautiful; dramatic colors moved with the sun across the rocks looming high overhead, and the bottoms of the gorges were enveloped in cool darkness. But nothing grew there; the earth and rocks were dusty and bare. The people loved it and its rugged beauty, but they longed for the softness trees and green growing things would bring.

Animals and birds living in the sunlight and shadows also wished for fertile ground. Lush plants, with green leaves, beautiful flowers, and fine fruits, would give shelter and better food for everyone.

The elders considered the matter, and decided to hold a great Corroboree to decide how they could bring trees and green growing things to their home. The people talked for a long time, and finally one man stood. He waved an arm toward the clouds in the blue sky, and said, "Beautiful trees grow up there in the sky. Can we knock down some of their seeds to grow here?"

The warriors thought this a fine idea and declared a great contest. All the warriors lined up with their best boomerangs, taunting each other with boasts of prowess; each declared he would be the one to bring the softness of green growing things to the Carnarvon Gorge. The line grew longer and longer; the sun grew hotter and hotter. The competition began.

One by one, with mighty throws, warriors sent boomerangs sailing into the sky, high above the heads of the crowds. Each brought wild cheers; then, as each vanished from sight, a silence fell as the crowd thought perhaps, this time, seeds would fall to earth in a shower of growth....

...Then a collective gasp as each boomerang returned, followed by—nothing at all.

Time after time this was repeated, till all the warriors had done their best. When the last warrior's boomerang had returned with no sign of seeds from the celestial trees, the crowd murmured in sorrow and disappointment. The Corroboree broke up; people moved away in twos and threes, shaking their heads and wondering what would become of their beautiful but barren land.

Before they could go far, one man so old his beard had turned the color of the white puffy clouds high above, where the trees grew in such abundance, said, "Why don't we ask Didane to throw his boomerang? His arms are so big and strong maybe he can do it."

In those days of the Dreamtime, when men and animals lived together in reasonable harmony, Didane the koala had the strongest arms. Even today, the koala's arms hold him aloft all day and all night in the tall gum tree that is his home, clinging to a branch, without danger of his falling. The others nodded, talking hopefully. A warrior was dispatched to Didane, who agreed to try.

Everyone gathered back at the Corroboree. Soon they saw Didane come into view, carrying his largest boomerang and accompanied by his animal friends. Kangaroos and wallabies set the pace for wombats and porcupines; a blue-tongued lizard crawled after them, glancing hopefully at the sky for signs of rain. It was a very hot day; the heat waves radiated up from the dry ground, and his blue tongue was very dry. The king brown snake slithered along behind them, trailed by a family of goannas. Even the green tree snake came, hoping his friend Didane would make it possible for him to have a tree to climb again. He was tired of living only on the ground.

The birds came in flocks, too, to watch such an unusual feat The red wattlebirds flew excitedly, chattering to each other all the way; they loved forests and were hopeful that their friend Didane could cause one to grow for them. The rosellas and pardalotes and fairy wrens came too, hoping for some sign that they would soon have trees to roost in. They arranged themselves so that they too could watch, and began to preen. The gang-gang parrots and cockatoos wanted the best view possible, so they soared up, up, and up, and fluttered back and forth as everyone below waited.

The people cleared a big circle for Didane. He walked to the center, gazed up at the sky and the beautiful trees that grew there high among the clouds, and then nodded to himself. He reached his strong arm back and then, with a mighty swing, hurled his boomerang high, high into the air.

The people gasped as Didane's boomerang sailed above their heads, above the whole Corroboree, and quickly flew above the beautiful birds that soared in the sky. The cockatoos soared in its wake, hoping to see where it went, and higher and higher they rose into the air. Up, up, and up the boomerang went, singing through the air, cleaving the clouds as it spun away, until it too vanished from sight as the warriors' boomerangs had. At last the gang-gangs had to drop back; it had flown much higher than they could. They landed near their friends.

Silently the people watched the skies; the animals watched too, Didane and the kangaroos and goannas and wombats who had come with him. For a long time they watched, and at last the people began to lose courage. Some began to cry at the thought that even Didane was not powerful enough to bring down the seeds they so desperately needed. And some began to walk away dejectedly, their heads low and their eyes on the ground.

But then there was a distant sound—the sound of a boomerang growing closer and louder. And there was another sound, too: the rustle and ping of seeds—seeds of all sizes and shapes, falling from the skies above to bounce and rattle on the ground as the boomerang returned. Didane had done it—he had brought seeds to the Carnarvon Gorge! Within moments the dusty and rocky ground was covered with a barrage of seeds, big, tiny, round, oval, in colors and shapes that the people had never seen before.

They all began to cheer and shout, and the kookaburra laughed with glee to see his friend's success. Didane had done what none of their warriors could do—he had gotten the celestial seeds for the people and animals, and now the earth would grow fertile and soft. As they gathered around Didane and began to celebrate, a soft rain began to fall, wetting the seeds and the rich earth alike, making all ready for the lush vegetation that would now grow from the heavenly seeds.

The Koala's Tail Ends in a Drought

In the days of the Dreamtime, when weather came and went, and men and creatures changed form and character quite often, the koala and the whiptail wallaby were very good friends. They lived cozily together in the same gunyah, and shared their meals as they shared the job of hunting out in the bush. They had one other thing in common: Both had long and beautiful tails, of which they were very proud.

They had been companions for some time when there came a terrible drought. Rain ceased to fall, and the ground grew hard and dusty. Water holes and billabongs dried up; creeks and rivers ran dry. The billabong near which they had camped became stagnant and nasty to drink, and the river that had fed it was dry as dust. The two friends missed the sweet clear water they'd tasted when the waters ran freely and the soft rains fell, but agreed that it was better than dying of thirst—as had happened to many other animals.

They stayed where they were for a while, watching with hope the shadows of clouds that filled the skies at sunset each night, carrying with them the promise of rain. But the clouds brought only empty promises that drifted away with the ending of the night, and in the morning the sun would beat down hard and hot, baking the earth and causing the little water that was left to disappear. And at last their own little billabong, foul as it had been, was dry. The two friends feared that their ends had come.

They had been mulling over this sad and sorry state of affairs for some time when the wallaby at last spoke. "When I was very young there was a drought as bad as this," he reminisced. "I was just a joey in my mother's pouch, but I remember it still. All the greenery grew brown and crisp, and the

birds fell from their branches. There were fights at the waterholes, and many animals died." He sighed at the memory. "My mother carried me everywhere, even though I was heavy; she crossed the mountains and sought out the bed of the river in the hope of finding water, but she was very weary and thirsty, and it took her a very long time."

The koala looked at him with interest. "What happened? What did she do?"

The wallaby shook his head. "A kangaroo happened along and saw us, and asked her why she bothered to carry me along. 'He is heavy, and you don't need such a burden at a time like this,' he told her. 'Leave him in the bush and come with me. I can take you to water, and we can travel much faster without him.' But my mother would not abandon me, and so the kangaroo left us both behind. His great leaps were two or three to my mother's one, especially when she was carrying me in her pouch, and soon he vanished over the dry horizon. But she just kept going, carrying me all the way, till she came to a river bed that was dry sand instead of dried mud. She went out to the middle of the riverbed and started to dig, and she kept digging till the hole started to fill with water—clean water." The wallaby got up. "We camped by that hole she dug till the rains came, and we had plenty of fresh water to drink. I'm going down to the riverbed now to dig a hole. Maybe I can find water the way she did." He sighed. "If we just stay here, we'll both die anyway; better to die doing something."

The koala was elated at the idea that they might be able to find water, and he said excitedly, "Yes! I will come with you. My arms are strong, and I can help you dig." They headed for the riverbank, but on the way they came upon some friends they had not seen since the drought had begun. The friends lay motionless on the hard cracked ground, and did not move; they were dead of thirst. When they saw their friends, the two companions became sad indeed, and sank to the ground beside their friends' bodies to mourn them.

As they sat, the wallaby became more determined than ever to find water, but the koala began to think of how tired and thirsty he was, and how sad and forlorn the bodies of their friends looked. At last they set off again, the koala looking back often toward the animals that had once been so happy and friendly. The two kept going and finally reached the riverbank, but the sun had baked them the whole way and they were both hot and weary. The koala suggested that the wallaby begin to dig, since he knew the most about it, and the wallaby agreed.

And so the wallaby set to work. He dug and dug and dug till he had a very deep hole, but there was no sign of water. He became depressed, and his arms and legs were very tired, so he asked the koala to dig for a while.

But the koala, who could not forget the images of their friends lying dead by the wayside, said, "I am feeling very ill and I think I might die. I would love to help you, but I don't feel as if I can right now. The sun is so hot and I feel so weak."

The wallaby felt very sorry for his friend and summoned up a bit more energy. He too remembered their friends, and how the kangaroo had hopped off and left him and his mother to die when he was just a joey. He went back to work, and at last he felt a cool dampness on his paws. Energized, he dug harder and faster, and at last water began to flow into the hole. Elated, the wallaby went to his friend the koala, who lay languidly in the shade of a dried-up bush. He nudged him just a bit, and said, "I've finally hit water, and I will bring some back to you."

But the koala, who had not been feeling quite as ill as he had let on, sprang up at this news and raced for the hole his friend had dug. He had to lean over quite far to drink, because the hole was so very deep, and his tail stuck straight up like the branch of a tree. The wallaby, at first so surprised at his friend's behavior that he did not know what to think, saw that tail sticking up in the air and lost his temper. He took out his boomerang and hurled it at his friend, and it cut off the koala's tail where it protruded from the hole he had dug.

And to this day the koala has no tail, as a reminder of his thoughtlessness and the wallaby's anger.

The Koala's Clinging Baby

Long ago in the Dreamtime, koalas were as beloved by the people as they are now. The people thought their cries sounded human and it moved them to compassion; they also loved the koalas for their gentle ways. Koalas were not hunted or killed or eaten, as were many other animals, and their babies grew up safely, able to wander freely without their mothers worrying for their safety.

One young female koala who lived at the top of a mountain would leave her baby each night to go down to the river where the bunyip lived. Now the people were deathly afraid of the bunyip, who had been known to kill people who bothered him. But the gentle little koala was not afraid of her friend the bunyip, and the two would sit talking under the stars about the earliest days of the Dreamtime until the night sky began to brighten into day and the dawn breeze would rise. Then the little koala would make her way home to care for her baby again as the birds woke to the sun. She would journey back up the mountain to the cries and songs of the rainbow lorikeets and the superb parrots, beneath the fluttering wings of the western rosellas as they left their early-morning perches to soar up to meet the golden daylight.

And sometimes the bunyip would leave his home by the river and climb the mountain to visit his friend the koala. She would find a soft comfortable place to leave her little joey, under the trees and beneath the watchful eyes of the Major Mitchell and sulfur-crested cockatoos, and together the two friends would go for long walks along the mountain paths, watching the stars and the moon and talking of days gone by.

The people who lived nearby were terrified of encountering the bunyip, and they would not go near the river at night. Then, when they found that the bunyip would sometimes leave his river home and go to the mountaintop, they became afraid of the mountaintop too. They were wary of the path the bunyip would take, and began to talk of ways to deal with the bunyip's nocturnal wanderings. They did not realize that the reason the bunyip left his home at night was to go visit the koala.

This alarmed the other koalas very much. They knew that the reason they were safe was that the people loved them and found them gentle and non-threatening, and they were very much afraid that if the people found that a koala was associating with a bunyip, the koalas might lose their special place in the people's hearts and would be in danger of being hunted and killed. So they went to the little koala and asked her to stop meeting the bunyip.

"But he is my friend," she said, "and he is no danger to us. The people will not bother us. No harm comes to them when the bunyip is with me. Surely they will realize that, and leave us alone."

The other koalas were not convinced, and they cajoled and argued and talked until the hour grew late. But the little koala stood firm. She would not give up her friend. By her reasoning, the people were safer when she was with the bunyip, so she was doing a good turn for the people; she had no wish to see anyone hurt. And when darkness fell, once more she found her baby a safe place to nestle, and off she went to see the bunyip.

After she left, the elder koalas held a council. "This cannot go on," they told one another. "She will endanger us all. We must find a way to stop her. What can we do?"

One koala spoke up. "The people's shaman has powers," he said. "We must watch him from the trees during the day and see how he works his magic. Then we can work magic ourselves and make our young friend abandon her dangerous ways." The other koalas agreed, and the very next day they set out to learn the shaman's magic.

No other animals were allowed to watch the shaman at work; the alert and cunning dingo and the kangaroos and wallabies, the cats and birds and snakes, were all driven off by the shaman before he would begin his rituals. He feared that they might steal his magic and use it against him or his people. But because the koala was so drowsy and sleepy, and because he loved them so, the shaman allowed them to remain. After all, where was the harm? They would see little; they slept so much.

But the shaman did not know that these koalas were alert and watchful through their sleepy-lidded eyes. They watched, and learned, as he put on his paint and did his dance and sang his chant and summoned the spirits. They saw how he made his magic, and how the spirits came and did his bidding, and they resolved that that very night they would work magic so that the little female koala would not bring doom down upon them all.

That night, the largest of the koalas waited till the little koala had set off to visit her friend the bunyip. Then he painted his face the way the shaman had, and he worked the magic just as the shaman had. The spirits came to him, and told him what he must do. So he went and gathered up the baby koala and held him close and cared for him till his mother came home. He whispered to the baby, "Cling to your mother and never let go," and worked his magic that the spirits had taught to him. The baby climbed onto his mother's back and held tight, and the little koala went off to care for him.

The next night, however, when she wanted to go visit her friend the bunyip, the baby would not let go of her. She tried and tried to get him to let go, and then tried to shake him off, to leave him in his safe little nest, but the magic was working and the baby would not let go. The little koala knew that she could not go so far as the river with her baby on her back, and regretfully she stopped visiting her friend the bunyip.

The magic worked so well that to this day baby koalas cling to their mothers' backs, to protect them from the people's fears about the bunyips. And to this day, the marks of the paint from the shaman's magic linger on the koalas' faces.

Koala and the Song of Sunlight

It had rained for weeks and weeks. Hunting had been difficult, and all the animal-men and -women came home soaked to the skin beneath sodden fur and feathers. But today had actually been sunny. The hunters had set out in bright sunshine for the first time in what seemed like ages, although the mothers with their young had stayed behind—hunting had been poor in the rain, and the mothers were having enough of a challenge to keep their children fed.

Mother Kangaroo had stayed at home in the big cave with the other mothers, although her Joey was getting too big, really, to stay in the pouch any longer. It was just too difficult these days to move around with him, and she knew she really needed to make him get out and walk on his own. He needed to learn independence so that he could start going on hunts with the rest of the adults as soon as he was old enough.

As she was thinking these very somber thoughts, odd for the long-awaited sunshine although appropriate for a gloomy day, she moved to the mouth of the cave and looked out in surprise. "The clouds are back," she cried to the other mothers. "Do you suppose they will make it home before the storm breaks again?"

"Oh, I don't know," Mother Possum said, adjusting the babies on her back. "I do hope so—or else I hope they can find some place to get out of the rain. They've come home every single day dripping, and it can't be good for them. If it keeps up much longer it will wash all the oil out of their fur and feathers, and then where will they be?"

Their conversation was interrupted by the drip, drip, drip of the first few raindrops. They looked out from the mouth of the cave, dejected, as the drips accelerated to a steady rain and then into a thundering downpour. The other mothers crowded around and they all peered out into the soggy gloom. "The poor dears," said Mother Quokka, who was smaller than Mother Kangaroo's Joey. "They'll never get home through this without getting soaked again."

"One of them will," piped up a small, wise voice from near the floor. "Mark my words." It was Mother Kowari, with her five babies clustered closely around her. Her dark eyes peered out into the dim, rainy afternoon as her slender nose twitched. "The Koala will be home soon, dry as a bone and looking every inch the gentleman." She sighed, remembering the bedraggled picture her mate had presented when he arrived the night before, his brushy little tail dripping all the way to their den within the cave. The Kowaris found the rain particularly distressing since, like the Koalas, they had no need to drink. All their liquids came from their food.

The other mothers all looked at each other and realized that the tiny Mother Kowari was right. Each night, when their own mates and the females without young came in looking sodden and completely miserable, Koala came in cheery and chipper, dry and tidy, fur soft and fluffy, almost as if he'd been freshly groomed.

"How do you suppose he does it?" asked Mother Goanna. "No one else can manage, even if they hide under a rock from the rains!"

"True," said Mother Ghost Bat from her perch overhead, looking down curiously at the others. "Do you suppose he hides in another cave during the day?" She thought for a moment. "If so, I must ask him where it is. My husband could probably hunt there...." Her voice trailed off as her baby demanded food.

Mother Emu said, "I know—if he manages to come home dry in this downpour, with that lovely fur looking so beautiful and dry, we must ask all the other hunters to follow him and see where he goes! Then they can come home dry too."

Everyone agreed that this was a good strategy, so they settled down to wait for sunset, when the hunters would be returning from their journeys.

When at last everyone came straggling in, every one of them was soaked to the bone. They dripped and shook themselves at the mouth of the cave, trying not to track in any more water than was necessary, and one by one filed in to greet their mates and young and to distribute any food they may have found.

All but one, that is. Koala came just a bit later than the others, entered the cave by himself, and was—as usual—dry and elegant in his fluffy coat of gray and white. His ears looked particularly splendid, with their long tufts of snowy white quivering delicately in the breeze.

"How does he do that?" wondered Mother Bandicoot as she watched him come in.

Koala, who was a bit of a joker, looked around at the others where they stood grooming themselves, steam rising off their wet fur and puddles collecting on the floor of the cave. His eyes twinkled knowingly, and he said, "Everyone all wet again? Pity, that." He blinked those intelligent eyes and wandered off to see his own wife and baby.

"That does it!" shouted Kangaroo, annoyed at Koala's casual attitude. Foraging in the rain was miserable work when done day after day, and he was tired of it. "I'm going to follow him the next time we go out in the rain, and I'm going to see where he goes. And when I do, then we'll all know how he keeps dry."

Sure enough, when the next day dawned cloudy and gray, with the promise of rain in the air, Kangaroo hung back in the cave till Koala had gone out. Then he left quietly and trailed after him. All went well enough until they came to a thicket. Kangaroo was far enough behind that he watched Koala go in, but when he hopped along to follow, he began to make so much noise in the underbrush that Koala heard him, stopped, and waited for him. "I don't know, Kangaroo," he said to the larger animal. "I think I'm just going to head home for a bit and wait out this weather. Care to join me?"

Poor Kangaroo could do nothing but follow Koala home to the cavern, and then venture out again alone—in the rain. Koala, of course, followed suit—later, of course, when there was no one to follow him about. And he returned that night as dry as ever, while the others had gotten caught once more in the late afternoon downpour.

The others were getting seriously annoyed at Koala's ability to stay dry and comfortable when the rest of them were getting soaked, so Goanna decided that he would follow Koala next time. Surely, he reasoned, he'd be quieter in the underbrush than Kangaroo with all his leaping and jumping.

But Goanna fared no better; he was able to avoid the bushes that Kangaroo hopped into, but as he glided along the ground he crunched along on twigs and sticks that made almost as much noise. Not only that, he splashed through puddles that Kangaroo had been able to avoid by jumping over them. He, too, returned crestfallen.

Even Kowari failed. His tiny feet didn't make much noise, but Koala's superb hearing picked it up—and Koala led him on a merry chase, going around in large circles that led circuitously back to the mouth of the cave. A dejected Kowari admitted defeat and went back inside.

Since Koala had to sleep so much, the others planned a secret Corroboree for the time when he would be dozing. Mother Possum spoke first. "Look at you all! You get soaked each time you venture out of the cave, yet Koala always returns looking immaculate and elegant. Surely one of you is clever enough to figure out how he does it, so that the rest of you don't have to go around looking like drowned rats." There was an indignant squeak among sudden turmoil on the cavern floor, and Mother Possum hastily apologized. "Nothing personal, Mother Rat," she hastened to say, and then added for the upset Rat babies' sake, "An unfortunate example. I was only using a figure of speech. Nobody's drowned!" Rat stepped forward to reassure his children, and at that the baby Rats finally settled back down, but Mother Rat kept a wary eye on Mother Possum just the same.

Although all were agreed that they needed to find a way to stay dry the way Koala did, no one had any more suggestions on how to do it or volunteered to try to follow him. They were all sure that with his keen sense of hearing and his beautiful fuzzy ears, he would hear them coming long before they ever got close—certainly dooming any attempt to sneak up on him. But then a strange little voice was heard over the throng. "I'm willing to try to follow him," said Beetle. "I can hide in places where he'll never see me, because I look like the bark of trees or the shreds of leaves on the forest floor. I can move through the bush almost silently when I fly. And I'm so small he would never think I could do it."

The others acknowledged the truth of this; in fact, they had forgotten Beetle and his family were there, because they were so small. Nobody really believed that Beetle could do anything, because they had never seen him fly—but now he spread his tiny wings and flew up to whisper in Emu's ear, "I know I can do this. None of you know me very well, but I can help." Kangaroo, who was close enough to see how high Beetle flew and heard what he told Emu, nodded.

"Perhaps our little friend can be the key to discovering how Koala keeps dry," he said to the others. "He is tiny and can fly silently. Maybe he can learn what the rest of us have failed to discover."

And so it was decided that in the next rain, Beetle would fly along after Koala to see how he kept his coat so magnificently dry.

Koala, of course, by now was looking for pursuers. But the next time it threatened rain, he set out as usual, listening with his magnificent ears and staying wary of what was behind him. Beetle, however, was as good as his word, and flew along from tree to tree in the bush behind him, staying out of sight and being as quiet as possible.

All went well, and Beetle stayed up with Koala. And then the rains came. Elated, Beetle watched to see what Koala would do next. He was surprised to see Koala climb a big, tall gum tree and clamber all the way to the top. Beetle spread his little wings again and soared up to a nearby branch to see what Koala was up to. He was very surprised to see Koala break two slender twigs from high, high up in the tree, and even more surprised to see him begin waving these two sticks in the air as if working magic. And then Koala opened his mouth and began to sing to the gray clouds gathered above.

Mr. Beetle clung to his perch on the gum tree and shook his head. Koala had a secret, indeed, but it was far grander than just staying dry in the rain! As Koala's voice alternately roared and softened in the song to the rain clouds, the clouds parted and drifted away. They left in their wake a bright blue patch of sky, through which the sun shone down cheerily on the one gum tree in the whole of the bush where the two creatures sheltered, one hidden and one perched confidently in the highest reaches of the tree. A bewildered and amazed Beetle watched in shock as the soft bright rays of the sun dried the tree's bark, making a haze of steam rise into the now-clear air, and shone softly on Koala's damp fur. Even the wind that had driven the chilly raindrops before it and made them all miserable changed to a soft warm breeze in the sunlight, driving the moisture from Koala's splendid gray coat and fluffing it gently until it was as dry as when he had left the cave.

Koala wasn't just Koala. He was the great Spirit Gundir, all-knowing and all-powerful, and his song was a song of magic and wisdom. His voice rose and fell as he sang to the clouds, and he waved his sticks in the air with the confidence of his whole being. Beetle watched in awe and fascination, not daring to move and hardly daring to draw breath. He saw Koala stretch and smile in the sunlight, then begin to gather gum leaves to eat and to take back to his family. Beetle stayed where he was, enjoying the feel of the warm sunlight but afraid some motion or sound might give him away to his powerful cave-mate. But at last Koala, tired from his efforts to sing the rain away and to gather food, began to get sleepy. His magnificent ears drooped and his head dropped to his chest, and he drowsed in the sunlight, content and warm.

When Beetle was sure Koala was asleep, and finally gathered the nerve to make his way back to the cave, he was overwhelmed with what he had seen and hardly knew how to tell the others.

"Oh, that is the most absurd story I have ever heard in my life!" laughed Bandicoot when Beetle finally summoned the courage to tell the others what he had learned. The rest of the animals began to laugh at the very notion. Sleepy, fuzzy Koala—the great spirit of Gundir! Such a thing was not possible, that a cosmic Being should live among the animals in secret. Koala himself pooh-poohed the idea, asking Beetle how it was possible that such a thing could be. Obviously, said Dingo, Beetle had been unable to find out the truth and had simply made it all up so that he would have something to report.

But Beetle, angry that the others did not believe him, offered to teach them all the powerful magic song that Gundir/Koala had sung to the clouds. Koala did not like this at all. That song was his and his alone, and he alone had the power to sing it—no other animal had the right to try to use his powers. The expression on his face changed from his usual sweet smile to one of aloof cynicism—and to this day he often looks this way. And from that day on, annoyed with himself for allowing Beetle to sneak up on him that way, he resolved never to let on that he heard anyone around him, so as never to be taken by surprise again.

Some animals grow still, the better to hear sounds around them, or cock their heads and twitch their ears, the better to gather the sounds they know are there. Others will flee in haste or go into hiding at the noises of pursuit. Koala alone will sit as if oblivious to all that goes on around him, pretending that he cannot hear the noises that betray activity. Yet this is his disguise, lest other animals learn his great secret—that he is Gundir—and try to steal his magical song.

The Sower of Discord and the War between the Birds and Animals

Long, long ago in the Dreamtime, all the animals and birds respected one another and lived together in perfect harmony. There were no struggles to see who might be the stronger or the swifter or the better, and everyone got along. And the people got along well with the animals. Many of each changed shape, in fact, so one could never be entirely sure who was truly a man and who was truly an animal—so everyone got along reasonably well.

However, there was one man who was an exception to this rule—as so often happens with almost every rule—and this single wicked exception made trouble among man and animal communities alike. Even more unfortunate for both creatures and men, he was a chief. This chief, who lived among the Aborigines in the Megalong Valley, had no such devotion to peace, as did the rest of his kind. In fact, he was a sower of discord, a master of deception, and he was known for stirring up arguments among his own people and between his people and others. His people, who trusted him as they trusted most other beings, often went to war at his instigation, never realizing that it was he who drove them to it or that he was never present on the battlefield except at the very back, to cheer them on and drive them to ever-greater deeds of battle as he reveled in the chaos and destruction that resulted.

However, at last their eyes were opened, and they saw that he was nothing but a master of deceit. Together they presented a united front and drove him out, refusing to fight or argue any longer

because of his nefarious influence. And when they had done this, peace was restored to their homeland, their new chief spoke peaceably with the other chiefs of other people, and the animals and birds once again came and went freely now that the sounds of battle no longer echoed throughout the bush.

Oddly enough, this did not bother the former chief unduly. Introducing fighting among humans had grown tiresome; they were so predictable and easy to deceive—partly because they were so trusting. Besides, he had discovered a whole new region in which to sow discord and promote fighting: the animal and bird kingdom. Into this united realm he determined to introduce distrust and enmity, and he had an ally in his efforts.

The truly sad thing was that this chief had one other great talent: He could make friends among the animals and the birds. He did not value this gift the way he should, however, and instead he resolved to turn it to wickedness. His only true friend was a beautiful bird, brown in color, with bright, intelligent eyes and a tail that was a splendor to behold. This bird was as smart as he was beautiful, and he could mimic the calls made by all the birds and even the animals. The chief took great pleasure in this talented bird, but he twisted the bird's gift as he had twisted his own to make him his single ally in sowing discord: He taught the bird to imitate the calls of all other creatures, whether they flew or walked or crawled. And then he encouraged the bird to use those calls to tease the other creatures, to mock them and send them astray.

In those days the animals and birds made only soft sounds—except for the dingoes, and the big Tasmanian tigers, who had fearsome cries, and the small spotted quolls, who made fierce, meow-like sounds; the birds whistled and sang soft, sweet songs. And the other creatures spoke softly. The koala made no sound at all in those days before discord, it is said, and the cry of the koala now is in imitation of another creature.

Early one morning a cry echoed through the bush. It sounded enough like a Tasmanian tiger that another tiger heard it and called back, then followed it, thinking that it was a fellow tiger. He made his way through the bush, boldly pushing through the underbrush, but when he got to where he thought the cry had come from, suddenly the call came again—this time from the side. He turned to his right and raced off in the direction of the call, but once again when he reached the spot the cry came again—it was behind him, in the direction from which he had just come.

Now the tiger was angry. He roared a challenge in response to the cry, and raced back the way he had come—and this time the only beings to be seen were the chief and the beautiful bird. The big creature paced back and forth as the cry came once more. Each time he pushed through the bush, checking each spot over and over, but each time only the chief and the bird were there.

The tiger at last backed away stealthily, growling softly, and retreated into the bush. He did not fear much, but he feared the chief. Too often he had seen how this man's people had been duped into fighting and even killing each other—and he knew who had done it. He had watched the chief at work.

On his way back to his den, the tiger met a wallaby, and told the little creature what had happened to him. "Have you seen another Tasmanian tiger?" he asked. "I have searched everywhere, but no matter where I turn I only see that chief and his bird."

The wallaby looked at him in surprise. "Why, I have been having the same problem," he replied. "I hear a voice like mine, and when I reply and go to look for her, there's no one there but the chief and his bird. How very odd!"

The tiger grew even angrier, and the insidiousness of the chief's influence made itself felt: Instead of going after the one individual who was truly responsible—the chief—the tiger resolved to avenge himself on the bird. Unaware of how his thoughts had changed to place blame where it did not belong, he was now convinced that the bird was responsible for the deception. He would put an end to the bird's trickery, one way or another.

From that day forward, he followed the chief and the bird everywhere they went. He watched and listened, and soon learned that the chief had taught the bird how to imitate everyone's calls and songs and speech. And he watched in disbelieving fury as the man and his bird deceived the other creatures, leading them all astray over and over and over again, and laughing to see their frustration and confusion.

The tiger had had enough. One day he saw his opportunity and pounced upon the bird, and although the bird flapped and squirmed and pleaded for its life, he killed it.

The chief, instead of mourning the talented bird, now used his own abilities even more to make creatures think he was their friend. His fingers traced strange patterns in the air; his arms captured the breeze and sent it forth with strange words in his melodious voice—his persuasive voice. All the birds of the air flocked to him, and when they were close by, he hurled his nullah through the air. It found its target and split the tiger's skull. The chief gathered the mockingbird into his arms and lifted it high in the air, displaying it so that all the other birds could easily see its wounds from claw and tooth. He bared his teeth and bent his brows, and the birds quickly picked up his anger.

A beautiful little mother koala woke from her doze when she heard all the uproar, and wondered what was wrong. She gently shook her baby into alertness, too, so that he would hold on tight, and she climbed down her tree as the baby clung to her back. She had no sooner reached the ground when another big tiger lunged at her. She was terrified, and for the very first time she cried out. Humans who were fearful had cried, and she had heard them; to this day the koala cries when it is afraid.

Another bird with greenish plumage had heard the mockingbird's calls, and from his perch high up in a tree he decided to try to imitate him. He called the great tiger in the tiger's own voice, and then, emboldened by his sheltered spot behind a great limb, began to call the tiger dreadful names. To this day this bird still calls in the tiger's own voice, as well as in that of the quoll; he does it so extraordinarily well that modern men have named him the catbird, because the quoll's cries—and the bird's imitations—so closely resemble the sounds of the cats that came to Australia long after the days of the Dreamtime. And to this day, the catbird keeps himself hidden away behind limbs and branches, the better to perform his deception. Nearby, the vulture-crowned leatherhead began to chatter and yammer continuously. He too still talks incessantly today, in the same chattering voice.

The kookaburra had sat through all this silently, not saying a word, only preening his brown and white feathers. But when the mockingbird began to speak in the tiger's own voice, he found it funnier than anything he had ever seen or heard—so preposterous was the sound of the fierce tiger coming from a small green bird!—and he began to laugh. Once he began laughing, he couldn't stop, and his laughter startled the cockatoos. They flew up from the trees in a burst of black and white, screaming for the very first time. Their screams frightened the little birds, blue splendid wrens and crimson rosellas, robins and tits and piping shrikes, and every bird that lived in the bush. They all cried out in alarm, and have never stopped since.

Now the chief saw his opportunity to make even more trouble. He took from the ground a mighty spear, and threw it with all his strength. His people, who had foolishly listened to him one last time, had been biding their time hidden away in the bush or crouching behind rocks. They took the flight of the spear as a signal, and emerged to use their own weapons, casting boomerangs and nullahs and spears and retreating to cover if they saw flung weapons hurtling their way. One of the boomerangs struck a huge gum tree and stuck fast, protruding as if in defiance of gravity, and the din was terrible.

In all this chaos the birds began to attack their former friends, the animals, to avenge the death of the mockingbird. They could fly overhead, dart in and inflict injuries, then soar high into the air to escape, and they began to win. But the animals, who were not inclined to take all these attacks without retaliation, resolved to turn the tide, and they began to climb trees in pursuit, following the birds into their aerie retreats. Even the snakes managed to twine themselves around the smaller trees and shimmy their way up to the birds' lofty perches. To this day many of the animals and snakes have kept this ability, with some wallabies and other animals climbing trees, and even snakes able to pursue prey high into the air on slender branches.

As the birds grew more and more tired from their desperate flights and bursts of speed, they began to fall from the trees; when they hit the ground the big tigers were waiting to snap them up and devour them.

The day, sorrowing at the turmoil beneath its rays, began to set at last and let the darkness hold sway. The flying foxes who had sheltered in the gum tree began to wake, for this was their time; so did the owls, who each night waited for the Big Man of the East to blow the rest of the light away.

Their keen night vision and sharp hearing took over and they spread their wings, dropping out of the trees, oblivious to the struggles that had gone on below them all day. They had not been among those deceived by the wicked chief, and they went about their own business.

Among the flying foxes, though, the very largest of them heard the cries and the battles, and resolved that he would try to do something to help his friends on both sides of the fight. He spread his broad leathery wings to drop from the tree and found himself stuck fast—the boomerang caught in the tree had snared his wing. He struggled and struck with his strong wings, and at last the boomerang fell from the tree, releasing him. He embraced the night air with his wings and soared away in pursuit of the setting sun.

The fighting continued below as he sped off; yet at last the people of the chief remembered, ashamed, that they had decided not to be led into any more battles by the chief's deceptions, and they retreated in fear and sorrow, watching with horror the fighting that they had never seen before as the birds and animals continued to attack one another. The chief stood by, well satisfied; he had sowed discord everywhere, and he acted as if none of it had anything to do with him. But he was laughing inside, and took it all in as if he had created a great thing of beauty.

The flying fox flapped his large wings, and soared on air currents that carried him with great speed through the starry night sky. He was desperate to reach the sun quickly, or else he must chase it all the way till morning. By then many more creatures and men would have died, and his heart ached at the very thought. At last the flying fox reached the sun, and crying out his plea to the light, he sank into it. At his touch, a brilliant beam of light burst forth and flashed straight toward the battle on earth. It blinded all the birds and animals with its overwhelming magnificence, and, terrified at their inability to see, they scurried for dark places to shelter from the strange untimely light. That is why today we now have birds and animals that can only see in the darkness, for the sun obscures their vision.

Other traces linger today of that tremendous battle, as reminders to all not to let it happen again. The gang-gang, which is gray of feather, bears a splash of crimson on its head in memory of a wound it sustained from a great tiger. It escaped, but the crimson-crested gang-gang cockatoo does not forget its fight in the great battle, and heeds its own reminder to fly away rather than do battle.

The corella and the redhead and, in fact, all other birds who sustained wounds and survived, to this day bear red or pink feathers, commemorating their roles in the fight. Even the flowers, such as the scarlet Doryanthes, onto which the gang-gang fell when it was wounded, is stained with the blood of the injured bird, and the flowering burrawang, which sheltered the bird as it finally died, is also tinged with the blood of the gang-gang in its red, red seeds. The epacris and the waratah also were splashed with the blood of the injured in the struggle, and although there are other tales to account for their coloring, the battle played its part.

Even today, reminders are everywhere across Australia of that terrible day, so that all the creatures of the land will know their history and remember its lessons. When birds, animals, and men look upon these brightly colored reminders of what can happen when suspicion and distrust gain the upper hand, all is well and peace reigns. But when they forget, times are fierce and sad, and the sun itself covers its face with clouds that weep in sorrow to wash away enmity. And if that does not work, then the sun burns fiercely down upon the earth to blind the fighters, so that they retreat and remember that life was intended to be lived in peace among all creatures.

Koobor and the Great Thirst

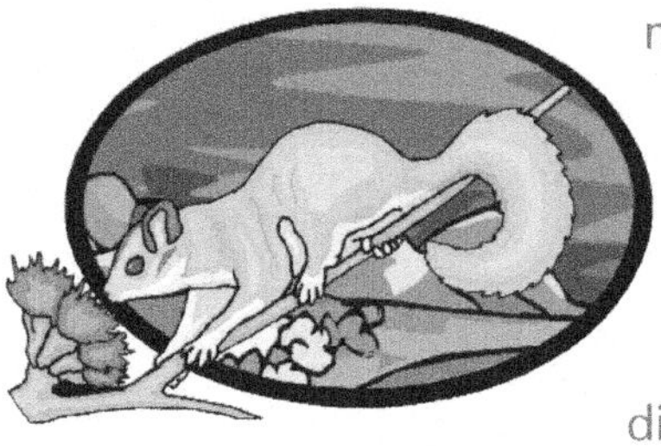

Long ago in the Dreamtime, when the animals had not yet taken their modern forms, but were still in the shape of humans, there was a sad young orphan boy named Koobor who lived with his extended family and friends near a stand of gum trees. The boy's family was cruel to him and neglected him often; he felt unloved and unwanted, and no wonder, for he was treated very poorly. One of the things his family did regularly to this poor child was to withhold water from him, so that he was always thirsty and never had enough to drink.

Koobor's family would head out to the bush each day to find food, and leave the child behind; he was young and small and would never be able to keep up with them as they roamed the bush looking for enough for everyone to eat. Each day when they left him, they would hide the water they had stored in buckets. Water was scarce and they had to protect what they had. So that in itself was not that unusual, but when they hid the water they would also make sure that even Koobor did not know where it was, so that he could not get a drink until they came home.

But one day they forgot to do this, and Koobor could hardly believe his good fortune. He would have more than enough to drink, and he could take the water that they had been so miserly with and store it up for himself. He found a young gum tree that had not yet grown very tall, and he hung the water buckets from its limbs.

Music is magic, and Koobor knew the secrets of music. So once he had hung all the buckets in the little tree, he climbed to a sturdy limb, made himself comfortable, and sang a magical song that

made the little tree grow and grow, so quickly that it was almost dizzying, till soon it towered high over the other gum trees and was the tallest in the forest.

While they were out gathering food, someone in the family remembered that they had forgotten to hide away their precious water, and in a panic they all headed back to the gum trees. But when they returned, they found Koobor high, high in the tree, far over their heads and completely out of their reach, watching the sugar gliders that had soared to the branches around him as they delighted in their new high roost. That would not have bothered them at all—but they realized that he had taken their whole water supply with him. Furiously they demanded that he come down and bring the water with him, but Koobor refused and clung all the tighter to the branch on which he sat.

"I have gone thirsty every day, so that my mouth has been as dry as the dust at your feet," he cried down from the treetop. "I could not even cry at your meanness, because I was so thirsty I had no tears. Now I have water and you have none, and you will see what it feels like to go without water and to be treated so shabbily—as you have treated me."

Although he was so high in the tree, the men knew they had to get water—and the water Koobor had taken was the closest. So they tried over and over to get him down from the tree, resorting at last to throwing things to try to knock him from his perch hidden high in the eucalyptus leaves. The cockatoos and rainbow lorikeets high in the other trees screeched at this and flapped their wings in fear, protesting not only on Koobor's behalf but for their own safety, and the sugar gliders, afraid of the shaking branches, left their holds on Koobor's tree and soared to other nearby branches. Taken aback at such a reaction from both birds and animals, the men stopped.

But they were desperate to get their water back, and so they resolved to try climbing the tree. Two or three of them sprang to it, and Koobor poured a bucket of the precious water down on them; the force of the water overbalanced them and they fell, wet and angry, to the earth. But after much conversation, one elder who was better at climbing than the others shimmied up the tree and caught Koobor in his high retreat. He struck Koobor again and again, to the others' cries of encouragement from below. So angry was he at the theft of the water—forgetting how shamefully he and the others had treated the boy—that in his rage he called Koobor a thief and knocked him to the ground, where his small body lay broken and still.

That shocked the others so much that they came to their senses. They stood in silence and realized what they had done to the small boy in their charge, and they were filled with horror and remorse. No one could move; it was as if they had all turned to stone. But suddenly they sprang back in amazement, for the body of the small boy began to change, growing even smaller and growing fur and large ears and strong arms with long clawed fingers. Koobor transformed into a koala and ran to the biggest tree around; he grasped the trunk with those strong arms and long sharp claws and climbed till he was far, far overhead, out of reach of even the best human climber. And even today that is the home of the koala, high above the heads of people, where he lives and no longer needs to drink water at all.

Because of the great wrong done to him, Koobor was granted the responsibility to make the laws. And for his very first law he decreed that the Aborigines could eat koalas, but they could not skin a koala or break any of its bones until they had cooked it completely. And further he decreed that if anyone disobeyed these requirements after they had killed a koala, the spirit of the koala would cause the land to dry up, so that a great thirst would descend on the people. The koala, of course, would survive, because he no longer needs water to drink. And because the koala lives alone, he would not be lonely and miss anyone who did not survive the drought.

And Koobor kept singing to the trees. It is said that if the songs of the koala in the night ever fall silent, then the trees will cease to grow.

Biographies

Storyteller **Lee Barwood** has been writing fantasy, environmental fiction, and mystery for over thirty years. Her stories and poetry have appeared in numerous magazines and anthologies, including *Ellery Queen's Mystery Magazine, Futures Mystery Anthology Magazine, Catfantastic III* and *V*, and *Horsefantastic*; her environmental novel *A Dream of Drowned Hollow* won Andre Norton's Gryphon Award. She has also worked as a magazine and newspaper editor, technical writer, and book and music reviewer.

Illustrator and editor **Joanne Ehrich** lives in San Mateo, California, USA, where she works as a graphic designer, with emphasis on print-, Web-, and user-interface design, and as an illustrator. She has attended photography trade school and holds a University degree in printmaking. Joanne has created numerous etchings, lithographs, and monotype prints, as well as paintings of animals and landscapes. She is also the author and editor of critically acclaimed *Koalas: Moving Portraits of Serenity.*

Founder of the Central Ohio Art Academy, **Donna Boiman** became a professional artist after taking two graduate degrees in science and working for ten years as a pharmacist. Currently the Academy's Director of Education, she also works as an artist; for her achievements in art and education, she has been included in four editions of *Who's Who in America*. Her art includes large-scale corporate paintings, and she has also won numerous photography awards.

The young artists from the Central Ohio Art Academy, whose work also graces these pages, are:

Helen Casebolt, who is from Pickerton, Ohio. She calls art her "passion," and is active in drawing, sculpting, and painting; she intends to increase her proficiency in all media. She also looks forward to channeling this passion to make her dreams come true.

Kelsey Darner, who not only pursues artistic goals in Pickerington, Ohio, but also hones her abilities in the study of biology and chemistry. She wants to use her love of science and animals to become a veterinarian. Long range, she hopes to be able to work at the Australia Zoo.

Jessica Littrell, who lives in Blacklick, Ohio. She loves music as well as art, and loves to travel as well as write. One of her sculptures rests in the office of Nick Bell, Educational Officer of the Australia Zoo in Queensland. She has also won awards for her artwork.

Jessica Motz, also from Pickerington, Ohio, who plays flute and volunteers at the Fairfield Humane Society. She also is a member of 4H, and shows rabbits in addition to working on art projects. She hopes to find a profession in which she can combine her love of art and animals.

Mariya Nudel, who was born in Tashkent, Uzbekistan, and now lives in Ohio. In 2005, she was one of the top winners in the Animals of the World art contest, judged by Nick Bell, Educational Director of the Australia Zoo. She created an original oil painting of one of Steve Irwin's favorite tigers and presented it to the Australia Zoo with the intent that it be auctioned to raise money for the Wildlife Warriors International program for tigers.

Stavroula C. Soulas, who lives in Blacklick, Ohio. Stavroula speaks fluent Greek, has traveled to Greece to stay in touch with the family's heritage, and is very proud of the way Greek artwork has influenced and inspired people throughout history. Eventually Stavroula hopes to be able to teach others about art and its richness.

Daniel Wiecek, from Pickerington, Ohio, who loves to draw animals and fantasy characters and to create sculptures. In 2002 he won a Lord of the Rings art show, judged by Tolkien artist John Howe of Switzerland, who worked with Academy Award-winning director Peter Jackson on all three Lord of the Rings movies. Daniel's other interests include kung fu and video games.

Illustration Credits

Donna Boiman: Pages 9, 17, 19, 21, 25, 31, 35, 47; **Joanne Ehrich:** Cover, title page, frontispiece, layout; pages 9, 15, 16, 17, 19, 21, 25, 27, 28, 29, 34, 35, 38, 39, 46, 47, 54, 55; **Helen Casebolt:** Page 31; **Kelsey Darner:** Page 8; **Jessica Littrell:** Page 47; **Jessica Motz:** Page 17; **Mariya Nudel:** Page 19; **Daniel Wiecek:** Page 21; **Stavroula Soulas:** Page 35. Providers for visual source assets used throughout include: Dreamstime, Fotolia, iStockphoto, Jupiter Images, and Lou Rozensteins.

Bibliography

Didane the Koala, by Grahame L. Walsh, illustrated by John Morrison, University of Queensland Press, QLD, Australia, 1985.

Koalas: The Little Australians We'd All Hate to Lose, by Bill Phillips, Australian Government Publishing Service, Canberra, ACT, Australia, 1990.

Koalas: Australia's Ancient Ones, by Ken Phillips, Macmillan, New York, NY, U.S.A.,1994.

The Way of the Whirlwind, by Mary and Elizabeth Durack, Consolidated Press Ltd., Sydney, NSW, Australia, 1941.

Some Myths and Legends of the Australian Aborigines, by William Jenkyn Thomas, Whitcombe & Tombs Limited, Melbourne, Auckland, Christchurch, Dunedin, Wellington and London, 1923.

Australian Legends, by C. W. Peck, Lothian Publishing Co., Melbourne, VIC, Australia, 1933.

Internet Sources:

www.sacred-texts.com | www.dreamtime.net.au | www.crystalinks.com | www.didgeridoos.net.au

Glossary

Bandicoot: A small marsupial with a long, narrow head and a long snout.

Bat: A nocturnal flying mammal.

Beetle: A hard-shelled insect.

Big Man of the East: A character in Aboriginal folklore who blew daylight away at the beginning of night.

Bilby: A type of bandicoot with large rabbit-like ears and keen hearing.

Billabong: A pool formed by a stream that can be stagnant or that flows only intermittently; a stream branch that dead-ends and leads nowhere.

Blue splendid wren: A small bird with brilliant blue plumage.

Blue-tongued lizard: A member of the skink family with a blue tongue that it displays when threatened.

Blue Ulysses butterfly: A magnificent intense blue butterfly native to Australia.

Boomerang: A curved shaped piece of wood that returns when thrown, used in hunting or as a weapon.

Brolga: A large crane, gray in color, with a featherless red head and gray crown.

Bunyip: Variously described as an evil spirit or an animal with a hairy horse-like head, a large furry body, and a loud bellowing cry, it was thought to live in billabongs or near water and to hunt people and animals.

Burrawang: A large palm-like evergreen tree.

Butcherbird: A bird with a beautiful song that lives in mangroves; its name comes from the way in which it kills its prey.

Carpet snake: A large non-poisonous member of the python family with characteristic markings on its skin.

Cassowary: This large, flightless bird with brilliant blue neck lives in the forest areas of Far North Queensland.

Catbird: A small shy bird with green plumage that has a catlike cry among its calls.

Cockatiel: These smallest of cockatoo birds have white or gray feathers, a yellow crest, and orange cheeks.

Cockatoo: A family of sociable Australian birds living in large groups; they have beautiful crested heads.

Corella: A white Australian bird with a colorful face and yellow underplumage.

Corroboree: A gathering, meeting, or council.

Crimson rosella: A colorful Australian bird and member of the parrot family.

Crimson-crested gang-gang cockatoo: An Australian bird with showy red feathers on its head; it is related to the galah and white cockatoos.

Crocodile: A large meat-eating reptile. It can swim and is quite fast on land.

Dingo: The "native dog" of Australia, the dingo is thought to have arrived between 3500-4000 years ago. It howls but does not bark.

Doryanthes: Also known as the Giant Spear Lily or Gymea Lily, this is a showy and large plant that is triggered to flowering by bush fires. Its blooms are red and spectacular.

Dreamtime: The Time before Time in Aboriginal lore in which all things were created.

Duck-billed platypus: One of two monotremes (egg-laying mammals) in the world (the echidna is the other), the platypus has a "duck's bill" and webbed feet and spends most of its time in the water.

Echidna: A monotreme (egg-laying mammal), the echidna is the oldest surviving mammal on the planet. It has spines similar to those of a porcupine and carries its young, once hatched, in a pouch.

Eel: A long, snakelike creature that lives in the lakes and coastal rivers of Australia.

Emu: A large (nearly six feet tall) flightless bird that can run very swiftly and swim extremely well.

Epacris: A plant of the heath family native to Australia.

Eucalyptus tree: There are over 600 native species in Australia, but the koala can only eat from about 36 of them. The leaves yield an aromatic medicinal oil.

Fairy wren: A small bird with spectacularly colored plumage native to Australia. It is related to the Blue Splendid Wren.

Fire ants: An ant, not native to Australia, that has a painful sting and lives in large colonies.

Flying fox: A member of the bat family, the flying fox is nocturnal and feeds on pollen, nectar, and fruit.

Frilled neck lizard: An Australian icon, this small lizard spreads its frill when threatened and runs about on its hind legs.

Galah: A beautiful, rose-pink and gray member of the parrot family native to Australia.

Gang-gang parrot: A redheaded member of the parrot family native to Australia.

Ghost bat: A small and rare Australian bat with gray and white fur that appears ghostlike when flying overhead.

Goanna: A large lizard found in Australia; it is a member of the monitor family.

Green tree frog: Bright green with red eyes and yellow feet, this frog is a familiar sight in Australia.

Gum tree: Another name for eucalyptus tree, and home to koalas, among other species.

Gundir: A powerful, great spirit figure in Aboriginal lore.

Gunyah: A rough or temporary shelter in the bush.

Joey: The young of a koala, or marsupial in general.

Kangaroo: A large marsupial mammal that stands on its hind legs and tail and hops from place to place. It carries its young in a pouch.

King brown snake: A large venomous snake common in the Australian desert.

Koala: A marsupial mammal, often called the native bear, with large furry ears and long claws for climbing. It carries its young in a pouch or on its back and lives in eucalyptus trees.

Kookaburra: A large member of the kingfisher family, this bird has a loud laughing call.

Kowari: A small carnivorous marsupial with a short brush-tipped tail and a pointed nose.

Lime green priamus butterfly: A spectacular brightly-colored butterfly native to Australia.

Major Mitchell: Also known as a Leadbeater parrot, this is known to be the most beautiful of cockatoos with magnificent white, pink, and yellow crest.

Marsupial: A mammal that rears its young in its pouch. Most marsupials live only in Australia.

Marsupial Rat: A marsupial resembling, but not related to, the rats of the rest of the world.

Mockingbird: One of several birds in Australia that mimic the calls of other birds. The largest and showiest is the shy Superb Lyrebird.

Mulgara: A small marsupial with a crest of black hair on its tail.

Numbat: A small marsupial that feeds on termites.

Nullah: A type of club or weapon.
Outback: The interior of Australia, a desert wilderness with with mountain ranges and widely scattered towns.
Parakeet: Also called budgerigars or budgies, these are small, colorful, friendly birds native to Australia.
Pardalote: A tiny Australian bird that lives in the eucalyptus canopy.
Pelican: A large black and white bird that lives near water and fishes for its food.
Piping shrike: Also known as the white-backed magpie, this bird is the symbol of the South Australian Government.
Possum: Related to possums in other parts of the world, yet different in appearance, these Australian marsupials often have furry tails.
Quokka: A small marsupial that resembles a wallaby.
Quoll: A spotted carnivorous marsupial with a shrill, catlike cry. It is also known as a tiger cat.
Rainbow bee-eater: A turquoise green and yellow bird with a black stripe across its eye, it really does eat bees.
Rainbow lorikeet: A very colorful, friendly, and playful bird native to Australia.
Red wattlebird: A member of the honeyeater family, this bird is large and noisy, and gets its name from the red wattles on either side of its neck.
Redhead: The short name for the Red-browed Firetail Finch, a native bird of Australia.
Robin: One of several native Australian robin species that includes the Flame Robin and the Scarlet Robin.
Rosella: One of several varieties of colorful Australian parrots.
Shaman: A medicine man or wise man among the Aborigines who works magic to help his people.
Skink: One of many lizard species native to Australia.
Starfish: A sea-dwelling five-armed (or more) creature that lives in the waters off Australia.
Sugar glider: A small member of the possum family able to glide between trees. It cannot fly, but glides on membranes that stretch between its front and back legs. Its name comes from its love of sweet things.
Sulphur-crested cockatoo: A large white Australian parrot with a sulphur-yellow crest and yellow underwings.
Superb parrot: A beautifully colored parrot native to Australia.
Tasmanian devil: A small, bad-tempered carnivorous marsupial, the Tasmanian devil is mostly black, with occasional white markings, and a short, thick tail.
Tasmanian tiger: Also called a thylacine, the Tasmanian tiger resembled a large dog with a long body. It had a big head, a stiff, heavy tail, and stripes on the back portion of its body. It is believed extinct.
Tit: One of several showy, colorful little birds, also called shrike-tits, native to Australia.
Vulture-crowned leatherhead: Also called the noisy friarbird, this is a bald-headed bird native to Australia.
Wallaby: A marsupial resembling a small kangaroo.
Wallaroo: A marsupial that is smaller than a great or red kangaroo but larger than a wallaby, with shaggy dark gray fur and a bare black snout.
Waratah: A beautiful showy small tree or large shrub native to Australia, with numerous small red flowers and red bracts.
Western rosella: A beautiful, yet shy, and extremely colorful member of the rosella family.
Whale: Any of several large seagoing mammals that inhabit the oceans off Australia.
Whiptail wallaby: A small wallaby with a long, thin tail, white-tipped ears, and a white face stripe.
Wombat: A small and shy furry marsupial that lives in burrows underground.

Published by Koala Jo Publishing
San Mateo, Ca 94401, USA
www.koalajo.com

Made in the USA
Middletown, DE
22 December 2020